A. C Ferguson

How they entered the harbor

and stories of the storm

A. C Ferguson

How they entered the harbor
and stories of the storm

ISBN/EAN: 9783744737272

Printed in Europe, USA, Canada, Australia, Japan

Cover: Foto ©Andreas Hilbeck / pixelio.de

More available books at **www.hansebooks.com**

HOW THEY ENTERED THE HARBOR

AND STORIES OF THE STORM

PART I.

Entering the Harbor of the Peace of God; or stories of the struggle with unbelief and the triumphs of faith and prayer in Christian Conversion.

PART II.

The Gleaner among fellow-voyagers, with introductory stories for each department.

DESIGNED AND EDITED BY

REV. A. C. FERGUSON

NEW YORK
A. D. F. RANDOLPH COMPANY
103 FIFTH AVENUE

AFFECTIONATELY DEDICATED

TO THE

YOUNG PEOPLE OF AMERICA, WHO

FIND THE SERVICE OF

𝕵𝖊𝖘𝖚𝖘

THEIR JOY AND HIS LOVE

THEIR DELIGHT.

PREFACE.

THE somewhat lengthy introduction for this little book seems an absolute necessity to properly explain and emphasize its plan, purpose and mission. Without doubt all true Christians recognize and appreciate the advantages derived from communicating to one another incidents of Christian experience, either in private or public meetings. Such incidents may be cheering, helpful and profitable by the witnessing of hearts together for the truth as it is in Jesus. Thus events which led to conversion, faith-victories over deep trials, finding joy in sorrow, a sweet draught from a bitter cup, answers to prayer, fulfilment of divine promises, special providences, joyous interviews with Jesus, times of rapturous love for Him, and His abiding presence are profitable to record and to communicate to others. The blessings thus imparted have been prized by myriads of hearts throughout the ages.

God's servants in ancient times erected memorial stones or altars in commemoration of special divine blessings, which were valuable as beacon lights in life's memories. At a later day, the recorded experiences of the Apostles became the sources of deep inspiration to faith, devotion and service.

The record of our Lord's earthly ministry is largely composed of accounts of His meetings with and service for individuals. He sometimes taught in the synagogue by the sea or mountain side, but the most joyous communion and rapturous experiences were enjoyed in personal interviews aside from the curious crowd. So to-day He goes with us in the shop, the store, the factory, the counting-house, the street and home, giving strength and whispering love and good cheer to every trusting, praying soul. It should be our privilege and pleasure like those who saw His face and clasped his hands, to record some specially blessed experiences with Him. There are some things we may consistently keep and ponder over within our hearts alone, as did His blessed mother after the angelic annunciation. We may not have angelic greetings, but experiences almost kindred to such interviews.

It is true in spiritual things, as in the natural relations of life, that the heart may have experiences within the realm of love, joy and sorrow, too sacred for mention, even to intimate

friends. As in natural relations, the
more pure and noble the soul, the
more judiciously will that soul guard
the Holy of holies where many of the
deepest, sweetest, most joyous or sor-
rowful experiences have lighted up, or
clouded its altars. I grant that this
may be emphatically true of one's relation to Christ in *many* experiences of
mercy and grace, even where spiritual
victories have been won, and where
we have met Him, in our Bethany and
Emmaus way.

But, these facts relating to experiences peculiarly personal in natural
relations should not be used to drape
or veil other experiences from the

vision of our fellows, where our
brother Divine has soothed us, bound
our wounds, thrust over us His shield
in greatest peril, and made us rejoice
amid the light and shadows of vanished days and years.

One of the greatest besetting sins of
modern Christians, like that of ancient
Israel, is to forget marvellous mercies
and deliverances even of the recent
past.   We see angels on our heavenly
ladders in our nights of deep personal
trials, and hide behind the shield of
the pillar of fire, like those distant rel-
atives of ours, and forget the en-
tire experience to-morrow.   Or, if we
have not completely forgotten said

experiences, we hesitate to tell a neighbor about them for *"various reasons,"* and vain excuses.

Every Christian is a monument of mercy and lavished love, and the voice of our Lover gently and sweetly speaks to us daily, saying—"Son, or daughter, *remember.*" That is an ungrateful soul which, being rescued from a watery grave, or a burning tomb, would fail for any reason to testify for and extol its Saviour. Its experience should not be too *"delicately sacred"* about such an event. Kind reader, do you agree with me? Should we not regard our spiritual mercies and victories in our relation to our Lord

in the same light? As every deed of
self-denial, of sacrifice, and of loving
service, registers itself in the soul by
its reflex influence, and thus enriches
the life and character, so all testimonies for Jesus, spoken or recorded
for others to read, may be as shafts
of heavenly light to win many a case
in the twilight or shadows of faith,
and be like a pierced hand or side
of positive proof, to some doubting
hearts.

There was one merit of the Greek
spiritual system which Christians of
to-day might well try to cultivate and
imitate. Their religion was insepar-
ably connected with the every-day

thoughts of the people. The artistic and social life of Greece was indispensable from her shrines and images. Thus, as all true Christians must know, the personal Christ in life and character is the only true ministry that wins by its living testimony. We profess to be ambassadors for Jesus Christ. An ambassador can most effectively represent his sovereign authority by recorded statements of his attitude on any question at issue. Even so, recorded statements of our attitude and experience to and with Jesus Christ may become living acts of the Apostles in this last decade of the nineteenth century amid the rushing, glowing and hopeful life of the young people of these times. Do we appreciate the advantages that may be derived by systematically recording the incidents of "life's storms" and an interchange of such records among friends. All spiritually-minded Christians, from the humblest to the most influential, have had experiences with Jesus worth recording as helps for others. There are unknown and untold victories won by the uncrowned heroes and heroines of the Church, which may light up many discouraged hearts, or become the battle-cry and final cheer to win many a hard-fought field in individual life.

The foregoing must indicate that the prime object of this book is an instrumentality for spiritual growth, by furnishing the means for inspiration in its recorded testimony, and thus influence the reader to "go and do likewise," by using its blank leaves to gather testimonies from friends young and old, in the societies of Christian Endeavor, Epworth League, Baptist Young People's Union, The Y. M. C. A., Salvation Army, and among the many bands of Christian workers throughout the land. It is conceded that the purpose of this book suggests an *innovation* in Christian habit, but I prayerfully hope that it may lead to the formation of what may be denominated TESTIMONIAL UNIONS OF SPIRITUAL COMMUNION.

These "Stories of the Storm," from living witnesses in widely diversified conditions, circumstances and spheres of life are not more especially marked than can be found in a large majority of Christian communities throughout the world. These records from persons widely known for their work's sake, or prominent position, are not of deeper interest or more valuable, than the testimonies from those, unknown to the world, who are living among the country hills or on the sea. All these of recent date were contributed to this book, while the others were gathered for a former edition, the endorsement of which by the public warrants the second attempt to thus render service for Christian hearts through its instrumentality. That it may be a gleaner among the multitude of young people and become a blessing is the chief motive of its designer and editor. Go forth then, "little Gleaner!" Be a messenger of our blessed Lord, exhibiting trophies of His grace, won in His name and by His strength alone. Be a lighted cross held before the eyes of fallen, wounded ones, who are looking up through their tears for the signs

2

of divine presence. Be the voice of our gentle Shepherd, speaking through human souls to many, saying : ''Lo, I am with you always!'' I shall be truly thankful if one heart traversing its lonely way, darkened and depressed, shall find herein light amid the shadows, imparting strength, comfort and cheer.

Yours, in '' His '' name and love,

A. C. FERGUSON.

BISHOP JOHN H. VINCENT.

I HAVE been asked to give a statement as to my religious experience; especially an account of my "conversion." I was born of a praying mother in the home of an earnest Christian father. Family prayer, morning and evening, was never omitted. Religious conversation, religious reading at the family circle, attendance upon all the means of grace, public and social, the singing of religious hymns and songs every Sunday evening for an hour or more

—all these means of grace brought
me into constant contact with religious agencies and the religious experiences of others. . The sense of sin I
always had.   A desire for goodness
was intense from my earliest recollec-
tion.   I was morbidly religious.   All
this religious conviction and aspira-
tion did not overcome the power of
selfishness and sin within me.   I was,
in spite of it all, although not an outwardly wicked boy, under the control
of impulse, selfish ambition and other
things not according to the Spirit of
God.   The great end I had in view
was "the certainty of future salvation."   I "sought religion" (using a

term much in vogue in those days in the Church in which I was brought up). I had many seasons of faith, peace and hope; many good resolutions; much private reading of the Scripture, and much secret prayer, but as I now look back upon my religious life in boyhood, everything was superficial, but I think sincere. I joined the Church "on probation" and in "full membership" when I was about sixteen years of age. There was very little difference between my inner and outer life before and after this act. As the years went by I lived a religious life outwardly, and my intentions and desires were of

the highest.   I had seasons of comfort
and many seasons of depression.   As
I now look at the most of my religious life, I believe that I was a *servant*
of Jesus Christ with mingled motives,
many humiliating failures and much
depression of spirits.   A few years
ago, after a period of profound and
unutterable mental and spiritual dis-
tress, I came into the light and liberty
of faith.   It was *the* crisis of my life.
A substratum of doubt and of evil, of
the presence of which I was con-
stantly conscious, but the destruction
of which most of the time seemed im-
possible, at the time of the crisis above
referred to, was apparently broken up

and the light of heaven seemed to reach the very foundations of my being. Since that time I have had no doubt whatever of my union with and allegiance to the Lord. For these few years I have walked in the light every day. Eternal things are as real to me as the Earth on which I walk, and the Sun that shines in the heavens.

JOHN H. VINCENT.

HARVARD UNIVERSITY,
    February 28, 1896.

FANNY CROSBY'S CONVER-
SION.

I WAS brought up under a religious training from the earliest moments of my life. My ancestors were deacons and choristers. I was brought up in the old Puritanic Presbyterian Church. I went to Sunday school when eight years of age, in Ridgefield, Connecticut. I always had a reverence for religious things, I think. I can date my conversion to a dream: I dreamed that a friend of mine was dying, and that he sent for me and asked me if I could give him up. I said, " No I cannot. You have always been my counsel and I cannot let you go." But he said, " Why would you chain a spirit to earth that longs to fly away and be at rest ? You know my loved ones are all there and I long to be in heaven." " Well, I replied," " I cannot give you up in my own strength." "Fanny," he said, ''will you make me a promise?" " Yes," I answered, ''anything in the range of human possibility, I will do for you." He looked at me earnestly, and said, "Will you promise to meet me in heaven ?" I said " Yes, by the grace of God, I will." He opened his large blue eyes, and looked at me intently and said, "Remember you are promising a dying man." I repeated the answer, the eyes closed, and the spirit passed away. I awoke, and for six months was under deep conviction. I could not think of anything but, "Will you promise to meet me in heaven?"

One evening at a protracted meeting in Thirtieth Street, I knelt at the altar feeling that if I was not saved that night I would never be. Prayers were offered, and the light began to dawn faintly at last. They began to sing that beautiful hymn, "Alas and did my Saviour bleed," when they came to the third line of the fourth verse, " Here Lord I give myself away," the burden was gone, and springing to my feet in the ecstasy of my joy, I cried out, " Halleluiah ! yes, Lord, I give myself away, 'tis all that I can do." The trouble was I had been trying to hold the world in one hand, and the good Lord in the other.

BROOKLYN,
March 15, 1896.

REV. C. H. SPURGEON.

Six years ago to-day (1858), as near as possible at this very hour of the day, I was "in the gall of bitterness, and in the bonds of iniquity," but had yet, by divine grace, been led to feel the bitterness of that bondage, and to cry out by reason of the soreness of its slavery. Seeking rest, and finding none, I stepped into the house of God, and sat there, afraid to look upward, lest I should be utterly cut off, and lest His fierce wrath should consume

28

me. The minister rose in his pulpit, and, as I have done this morning, read this text : "Look unto Me, and be ye saved, all the ends of the earth : for I am God, and there is none else." I looked that moment ; the grace of faith was vouchsafed to me in the self-same instant ; and now I think I can say with truth :

> " E'er since by faith I saw the stream,
>   His flowing wounds supply,
>   Redeeming love has been my theme,
>   And shall be till I die."

I shall never forget that day while memory holds its place ; nor can I help repeating this text when I re-member that hour when first I knew the Lord. How strangely gracious !

How wonderfully and marvelously kind, that he who heard these words so little time ago for his own soul's profit, should now address you this morning as his hearers from the same text, in the full and confident hope that some poor sinner within these walls may hear the glad tidings of salvation for himself also, and may to-day, on this 6th of January, be "turned from darkness to light, and from the power of Satan unto God!"

MISS FRANCES E. WILLARD.

I was lying on my bed in my home at Evanston, Illinois, in the crisis of typhoid fever. It was one night in June, 1859. The doctor had said that the crisis would soon arrive, and I had overheard his words. Mother was watching in the next room. My whole soul was intent, as two voices seemed to speak within me, one of them saying: "My child, give me thy heart. I called thee long by joy, I call thee now by chastisement; but

I have called thee always and only
because I love thee with an everlasting love." Solemnly, definitely, and
with my whole heart I said, not in
spoken words, but in the deeper language of consciousness : "If God lets
me get well, I'll try to be a Christian
girl." I was then nineteen years old.
But this resolve did not bring peace.
"You must at once declare this resolution," said the inward voice. After a
hard battle, in which I lifted up my
soul to God for strength, I faintly
called mother from the next room, and
said "Mother, I wish to tell you that
if God lets me get well, I'll try to be a
Christian girl." She took my hand,

knelt beside by bed, and wept and prayed. I then turned my face to the wall and sweetly slept. That winter we had revival services in the old Methodist church at Evanston. Dr. (now Bishop) Foster, was president of the university, and his sermons, with those of Drs. Dempster, Bannister and others, deeply stirred my heart. The very first invitation to go forward, kneel at the altar and be prayed for, was heeded. For fourteen nights in succession I thus knelt at the altar, expecting some utter transformation. One night when I returned to my room, baffled, weary and discouraged, and knelt beside my bed, it came to

3

me quietly that this was not the way ;
that my "conversion," my "turn-
ing about," my religious experience
(religio, to bind again), had reached
its crisis on that summer night when
I said "yes" to God.   A quiet certi-
tude of this pervaded my consciousness, and the next night I told the
public congregation so, gave my
name to the church as a probationer,
and after holding this relation for a
year—waiting for sister Mary, who
joined later, to pass her six months'
probation—I was baptized and joined
the church "in full connection."

COWPER, THE POET.

Cowper, the poet, speaking of his religious experience, says :

"The happy period which was to shake off my fetters and afford me a clear opening to the free mercy of God in Christ Jesus, was now arrived. I flung myself into a chair near the window, and seeing a Bible there, ventured once more to apply to it for comfort and instruction. The first verse I saw was the 25th of the third chapter of Romans: 'Whom God hath set forth to be a propitiation, through faith in His blood, to declare the righteousness for the remission of sins that are past, through the forbearance of God.' Immediately I received strength to believe, and the full beams of the Sun of righteousness shone upon me. I saw the sufficiency of the atonement He had made, my pardon sealed in His blood, and the fullness and completeness of His justification. In a moment I believed and received the Gospel."

REV. CHARLES WESLEY.

Charles Wesley had been for years groping in spiritual darkness—

"Without one cheering beam of hope,
Or spark of glimmering day."

On a bright morning in May, 1738, he awoke, wearied and sick at heart, but in high expectation of the coming blessing. He lay on his bed "full of tossings to and fro," crying out : "O Jesus, Thou hast said : 'I will send the Comforter unto you.' Thou art God, who canst not lie. I wholly rely upon Thy promise. Accomplish it in Thy time and manner." A poor woman, Mrs. Turner, heard his groaning, and, constrained by an impulse never felt before, put her head into his room, and gently said: "In the name of Jesus of Nazareth, arise and believe, and thou shalt be healed of all thine infirmities." He listened, and then exclaimed: "Oh, that Christ would but thus speak to me!" He inquired who it was that had whispered in his ear these life-giving words. A great struggle agitated his whole man and in another moment he exclaimed earnestly: "I believe! I believe!" He then found redemption in the blood of the Lamb, and experienced the forgiveness of sins. The hymn he wrote to commemorate the anniversary of his spiritual birth, shows the mighty change that had taken place, and is best expressed in his own language :

"O, for a thousand tongues to sing!"

A SLAVE'S.

CAMBO, a negro slave, gave the following account of his conversion : "While in my own country (Guinea), me had no knowledge of the being of a God ; me thought me should die like the beasts. After me was brought to America, and sold as a slave, as me and another servant of the name of Bess was working in the field, me began to sing one of my old country songs, 'It is time to go home ;' when Bess say : 'Cambo, why you sing for ?' Me say : 'Me no sick, me no sorry, why me no sing ?' Bess say : 'You better pray your Lord and Massah to have mercy on your soul.' Me looked round, me looked up, me see no one to pray to ; but the words sound in my ears, 'Better pray to your Lord and Massah.' By and by me feel bad, sun shine sorry—birds sing sorry—land look sorry, but Cambo sorrier than all. Then me cry out : 'Mercy, mercy, Lord! on poor Cambo !' By and by water come in my eyes, and glad come in my heart. The sun look gay, woods look gay, birds sing gay, but poor Cambo gladder than them all. Me love my Massah some ; me want to love him more."

ORIGEN.

ORIGEN, who was born in Alexan dria eighteen years after Polycarp's death, and who became one of the most earnest and influential of the Christian fathers, was early instructed by his mother in the Christian religion, and to her he owed, under God, both his religion and his greatness.

REV. DR. JOHN HALL.

I HAD the great blessing, from the God of Salvation, of instruction from my infancy in the truths of God's word. I could not indicate a *time* of conversion. At the age of fourteen I was received as a member of the Church, after careful examination by a faithful pastor, who drew out my convictions as to my confidence in Christ as my Redeemer, my purpose to do His will as it was set forth in His word, and my right understanding of the nature and efficacy of the Sacraments.

43

ABRAHAM LINCOLN.

ABRAHAM LINCOLN believed in the Christian Religion, and revered God before he became President of the United States, as was evinced by his request to his friends and neighbors at Springfield, Ill., on his departure for Washington, to be inaugurated. He said : "Pray for me that I may have God's help, and that he may guide me in the discharge of the great responsibilities I am about to assume." During the first half of the war, his

little son "Tad" became a conspicuous figure at the Executive Mansion.
He was a sunny, promising child, and
the especial comfort and delight of his
father's heart amid the dark days, and
cares of state. It became well known
that " Tad Lincoln " had the run of the
White House, and was on familiar
terms with the great men of the land.
While Generals and Senators were waiting for hours to obtain an interview with
the toiling President, "Tad" would be
seen frequently going to and from the
almost sacred presence of his father,
when men on whose acts momentous
events might depend, were anxiously
seeking the favors the little boy so

freely enjoyed. So it came to pass,
that some of these men whose duties
were particularly pressing, more than
once took advantage of "Tad's"
presence, and by him sent a special
message to his father, that they must
see him at once. Undoubtedly the
great-hearted President was not dis-
pleased with the spirit of this little
ruse, for he responded to these particular messages. Little "Tad" was
taken violently sick and the President,
amid all his anxieties and burden-
bearing, tenderly watched his sick
child in vain, as God called the little
one home. "Tad's" death was a
crushing blow to Lincoln's heart, but

it brought him nearer to God in Jesus' love. His son had been an intercessor for others to him. Said Lincoln : "I now feel the force of the Scripture that saith : 'God so loved the world that He gave His only begotten Son, that whosoever believeth in Him should not perish, but have everlasting life.' I now see as never before the preciousness of God's love in Jesus Christ, and how we are brought near to God as our Father by Him." Thus was Lincoln's saving faith in Christ declared to the world.

GELASIUS, AN ACTOR.

Gelalius was a comic actor in the
theatre at Heliopolis. A burlesque of
Christian ordinances was one day
given for the entertainment of the
heathen audience. A large bath-tub
was placed on the stage filled with
warm water. In this Gelasius was
dipped by the other actor, who pro-
nounced over him the usual formula :
" I baptize thee in the name of the
Father, and of the Son, and of the Holy
Ghost." When he came forth he was

arrayed in white, after the custom with the newly baptized. A great change was observed in his appearance. His jesting air was gone, and his face wore a look of deep seriousness. He announced his conversion, saying : "I am a Christian. I will die as a Christian." When they heard this, and understood that he was in earnest, the mob rushed upon the stage, seized him, dragged him forth in his white robe and stoned him to death. A. D. 297.

4

REV. DR. A. C. DICKSON.

I was converted at eleven years of age. I had read Bunyan's "Pilgrim's Progress" and thought that I must have a burden as heavy and large as Pilgrim's pack. Suddenly it would fall off and I would go on to heaven singing and shouting. I was burdened because I was not burdened ; I wept because I could not weep. In that state of mind I heard a gospel talk on the text "Believe on the Lord Jesus Christ and thou shalt be saved." I said to myself,

That does not say be burdened or un-
burdened; it says one thing, " Believe." I determined to do just that
and quit seeking anything more.
There came into my heart a quiet
peace but no ecstasy. I accepted the
Lord Jesus Christ in cold blood by an
act of simple faith, and that text has
been my sheet anchor ever since.
Times of ecstatic joy have come, but
I do not put much value on them.
Jesus Christ, author and finisher of
faith, is all and in all.

REV. ALFRED COOKMAN.

ALFRED COOKMAN was converted at the age of ten years. His father was the pastor of the Methodist Episcopal Church at Carlisle, the seat of Dickinson College. Much spiritual interest had been awakened among the students. On one occasion many of them bowed at the altar, and no little interest was naturally felt in their behalf. It was hardly possible to overestimate the amount of good that might result from the personal consecration of these educated young men to the Master's service. But in that congregation, quite overlooked, attracting only the particular attention of the Christian person at the time, was one little lad, not yet twelve years of age. He did not make himself conspicuous by the position he took, or by any marked demonstration of feeling on his part, but in a distant corner of the church, kneeling alone, he wept and prayed earnestly, and cried: "Precious Saviour, thou art saving others, oh! wilt thou not save me?" There was a pious elder in the Presbyterian church in Carlisle who was present. With a warm heart and with gentle words he unfolded, to the faith of the weeping boy, the simple and wonderful plan by which God saves us, when we trust in Him who died for us, as our Saviour. "I will believe," the sobbing child responded; "I do believe. I now believe that Jesus is my Saviour, that He saves me—yes, even now." And faith, in the trusting boy, brought its promised result of peace and love and joy. Many years after, as he recurred to this hour, he writes: "I love to think of it; it fills my heart unutterably full of gratitude, love and joy. 'Happy day, oh! happy day, when Jesus washed my sins away.'"

REV. DR. RUSSELL H. CONWELL.

" It is interesting to note that the work of the distinguished preacher at the Baptist Temple in Philadelphia, Russell H. Conwell, can be traced back to the influence of a little boy by the name of Ring, who went to the war with Mr. Conwell in the Second Massachusetts Regiment. Mr. Conwell at jail, was a professed disbeliever in the Bible and openly expressed his views, but this little boy from Westfield, Mass., went out with Captain Conwell as his servant under military discipline. The boy was a true Christian and had promised his mother before her death that he would read the Bible every day. Captain Conwell often ridiculed him for his religious fervor, but the boy was true to his Bible. During a battle at Newport, N. C., when the Union troops were driven across the Newport river, a long railroad bridge was set on fire to prevent the enemy from following. Captain Conwell's gold-sheathed sword, which was presented to him at the city of Springfield, Mass., was overlooked in the excitement and left in his burning tent. Captain Conwell used another sword and kept the pres-

ent carefully wrapped in his tent.
The boy, after the bridge was blazing,
thought of the sword and ran back for
it. He secured it in the midst of the
enemy and succeeded in carrying the
sword through the smoke and fire of
the burning bridge, but it cost him his
life, and his dying words were, Tell
the captain I love him, and I hope he
has got his sword." Afterward Col.
Conwell was wounded severely, at
Kennesaw Mountain in Georgia, and
left upon the field. He expected to
die. The next day he was carried un-
conscious to the hospital tent, and
when he recovered his consciousness
he thought of the boy who had saved

his sword and felt the need of his prayers. Col. Conwell sent for the chaplain and told him of the boy's sacrifice to save his sword and of his resolution made the night before that if he should live, he would himself be a Christian. He gave his heart to Christ that day and at the close of the war, united with the First Baptist Church in St. Paul, Minn."

PETER JACOBS, AN INDIAN.

THE following is the experience of Peter Jacobs, a Chippewa Indian of Canada, as given at Exeter Hall, London : "When I was in my heathen state, I heard a missionary speak of a beautiful heaven where nothing but joy was to be experienced, and of the awful flames of hell into which the wicked shall be cast if they do not believe in the Lord Jesus Christ. I made inquiry if there was any possibility of a Chippewa Indian getting into heaven. I was told that heaven was open to all believers in Christ Jesus. I was very glad when I understood this; I began to pray. I said: 'O Christ, have mercy on me, a poor sinner, poor Indian!' This was the beginning of my prayer, and the end of my prayer. I could not say any more, because I did not know any more English. I thought if I prayed in Chippewa, Christ would not understand me. Christ affected my heart very much. I felt just like a wounded deer. When we shoot a deer in the heart with bow and arrow, he runs away as if he was not hurt; but when he gets to the hill, he feels the pain, and lays down on that side where the pain is most severe. Then he feels the pain on the other side, and turns over, and so he wanders about till he dies. I then went up into a stable where hay was kept, and there I prayed: 'O my Heavenly Father, now have mercy upon me, for the sake of Thy son Jesus Christ.' I then prayed again: 'O Jesus, the Saviour of the world, apply now Thy precious blood to my heart, that all my sins may depart!' I wanted rest and sleep, but I could not rest. Like the wounded deer, I turned from side to side, but I could not rest. At last I got up at midnight and walked about my room : I made another effort to pray and said : 'O Jesus, I will not let Thee go until Thou bless me,' and before the break of day I found that my heavy heart was taken away, and I felt happy ; I felt the joy which is unspeakable and full of glory. Then I found Jesus was sweet indeed to my soul."

CHARLES CULLIS, M. D.

CHARLES CULLIS, of the Faith Home, of Boston, says :

"At about the age of seventeen, I felt I ought to be a Christian. How, I did not know. Nobody told me. I supposed the only way would be to read the Bible and pray, and I went at it. When I was converted, I do not know, but I am very sure I was. I don't know the date, for there was no particular sensation or emotion to mark it. Some four or five years after, I met with a great sorrow, and I consecrated myself wholly to God. Soon after I thought about doing something for the Master, and it came about in answer to prayer, in the establishment of a Consumptives' Home, and other institutions. My thought then was, how to conduct this work— whether or not I should beg. The promises of God were brought very forcibly to my mind as to whether they were true or not. I puzzled over them for a few days, until I was led to declare: 'I will believe every word of God's truth.' From that moment to this I have never had the least shad-

ow of doubt of the truths of God's
word, and have acted upon the promises and lived according to them for
nearly twenty-five years."

5

REV. JOHN NEWTON.

JOHN NEWTON when a young man was captain of a Liverpool vessel, and was engaged in the slave trade during a number of years. But he learned to pray at his mother's knee. She was taken to heaven before he was eight years old. At sea in the midst of many dangers, and much wickedness, his agonizing prayer was often (when under temporary conviction of sin) : "My mother's God, the God of mercy, have mercy on me!"

He was engaged to be married to an estimable young Christian lady of London. On one occasion he called to bid her good-bye in the evening as his ship was to sail for the African Coast the following day. As he was parting from his love, she pleaded with him to abandon the business in which he was engaged.

He replied : "At this hour (eleven o'clock) to-morrow night, I shall be many leagues at sea. You see yonder North Star—will you look at that star at this hour to-morrow night and pray God to help me to do His will? I will call on His name while gazing at the star, and thus we will pray and be together." IIis prayers to his mother's God were heard, and his mother's prayers were answered. Through him, Scott the Commentator was led to Christ, and Wilberforce, the champion of African freedom, and author of that "Practical View of Christianity," which brought Leigh Richmond into the ministry of Christ.

When Newton was an old man, while standing in the doorway of his home one day, he saw a drunken man passing in the street and cursing God and men—said he: "There goes John Newton, but for the *grace of God.*"

POLYCARP.

Polycarp was the disciple and intimate friend of the apostle John, and suffered martyrdom A. D. 165, having enjoyed the personal instruction of John about twenty-three years.

He was a glorious example of the power of early instruction and the sanctification of childhood. Polycarp was Bishop of Smyrna. When ninety years old he was brought to the stake, for no other crime than that of being a Christian.

MARTIN LUTHER.

Luther, in speaking of his conversion, said : "If ever there was a man who, before the gospel was made known to him, highly esteemed the teachings of the fathers and the decrees of the Pope, and with great earnestness contended for the same, then it was I who did so in a peculiar manner. And yet, no matter how much I studied and prayed, I found no peace to my soul." One day while studying his Bible, his eyes fell upon the passage : "The just shall live by faith." Alone it was incom-

prehensible. These words involved
the perplexity of terror. Defined in
their narrow meaning and without col-
lateral significance, even now they
carry an impression of austerity. So
Luther read them in his Bible. He
turned to the friendly commentary of
St. Augustine, read it and made a note.
He said: "Then was I glad; for I
learned and saw that God's righteousness was His mercy, by which He accounts and holds us justified. Thus I
reconciled justice with justification,
and felt assured that I was in the true
faith. It seemed to me as though
heaven's gate stood fully open and I
was entering therein."

" I WAS a child of teaching and prayer; I was reared in the household of faith; I knew the catechism as it was taught; I was instructed in the Scriptures as they were expounded from the pulpit and read by men , and yet, till after I was twenty-one years old, I groped without the knowledge of God in Christ Jesus. I know not what the tablets of eternity have written down, but I think that when I stand in Zion, and before God, the

brightest thing which I shall look back
upon will be that blessed morning of
May when it pleased God to reveal to
my wandering soul the idea that it was
His nature to love a man in his sins
for the sake of helping him out of them ;
that He did not do it out of compliment
to Christ, or to a law, or a plan of salvation, but from the fullness of His
great heart ; that He was a Being, not
made mad by sin, but sorry ; that He
was not furious with wrath toward the
sinner, but pitied him—in short, that
He felt toward me as my mother felt
toward me, to whose eyes my wrong-
doing brought tears, who never pressed
me so close to her as when I had done

wrong, and who would fain, with her yearning love, lift me out of trouble. And when I found that Jesus Christ had such a disposition, I felt that I had found a God. I shall never forget the feelings with which I walked forth that May morning. The golden pavements will never feel to my feet as then the grass felt to them ; and the singing of the birds in the woods—for I roamed in the woods—was cacophonous to the sweet music of my thoughts ; and there were no forms in the universe which seemed to me graceful enough to represent the Being, a conception of whose character had just dawned upon my mind. I felt when I had,

with the Psalmist, called upon the
heavens, the earth, the mountains, the
streams, the floods, the birds, the
beasts, and universal being, to praise
God, that I had called upon nothing
that could praise Him enough for the
revelation of such a nature as that in
the Lord Jesus Christ."

"Yes, it was on Advent Sunday, December 2, 1873, I first saw the blessedness of *true* consecration. I saw it as a flash of electric light, and what you see you can never unsee.

"There must be full surrender before there can be full blessedness. God admits you by the one into the other. He, Himself, showed me all this most clearly. First, I was shown that "the blood of Jesus Christ His Son cleanseth us from all sin," and

76

then it was made plain to me, that He who had thus cleansed me, had power to keep me clean. So I just utterly yielded myself to Him, and utterly trusted Him to keep me."

BALLINGTON BOOTH.

THE following facts of the conversion of Ballington Booth and of his wife, Mrs. Maud Booth, like other accounts were especially contributed for " How They Entered the Harbor."

Commander Booth was born in the town of Brighouse, Yorkshire, England, on the 28th of July, 1857, and is the second son of General William Booth and his late wife Catherine. Being reared from infancy under the influence of a pious father and mother,

he was converted when a child. He
was a delicate and sensitive child;
tall, thin, intensely high-strung ; and
for many years it was evident that he
had outgrown his strength. But he began the work which he has carried out
so characteristically, consistently, and
successfully through his life, in his
early boyhood. He began conducting
little meetings on the playground, and
was often struck and knocked down
by schoolmates who took issue with
him. His first serious work was
undertaken in Manchester, England,
when he had attained the rank of
Captain in the Salvation Army. During his work there he was arrested and

imprisoned; so violent was the opposition to the methods of the Army, at that time. He was treated as a common felon, given prison clothes and prison diet. This, however, far from quelling his enthusiasm and stopping the work, only acted as a further incentive to Captain Booth and his brave assistant; and brought thousands to hear him who otherwise would have ignored his appeal.

Captain Booth became Major Booth, then Colonel Booth, father of the first Training Home in 1880. His grand and successful work in America during the last ten years has won the admiration of all true lovers of our Lord.

MRS. BALLINGTON BOOTH.

Mrs. Ballington Booth is the daughter of the Rev. Samuel Charlesworth, a rector of the Church of England. This youngest of his three children, was born at Lympsfield, near London. Three years after her birth, Mr. Charlesworth was given charge of a large and important parish in the East End of London. It is rather a singular coincidence that the "penny gaff" which the Rev. William Booth had captured for his mission was just opposite the church in which Mr. Charlesworth preached; and still more singular that when the police drove Mr. Booth from the streets the Rectory gates were thrown open, and upon those grounds were held many successful open-air meetings.

Her mother, too, was one who made the people's interests her own, and in their parish no one was so reverenced and loved for kindly deeds and cheering words as the Rector's wife. It was her indefatigable toil and self-sacrifice for others that shortened her life by many years, and brought to Maud Charlesworth a loss that was irreparable. Mrs. Charlesworth had frequently taken her little girls across to Mr. Booth's mission, and it was no surprise nor disappointment to her when her youngest daughter consecrated herself to God in one of those meetings.

Shortly after her mother's death, at the age of seventeen, Maud Charlesworth, accompanied by her father, crossed to France to begin an active warfare by the side of Catherine Booth the General's eldest daughter, amid the darkness and infidelity of Paris. Two years in warfare which still counts as the most difficult and bitter in Salvation Army history, made of the timid girl a tried veteran. Her consecration and devotion to Christ are well known.

FRANCIS E. CLARK-

LIKE a great multitude of youth I was born into a Christian home and brought up by Christian parents. I always knew what my duty was from the earliest day that I can remember; and when I have not done that duty it has not been for lack of knowledge but for lack of will and determined purpose. I always knew that I ought to be a confessed Christian, and cannot remember the time when any

85

other course seemed to be right or reasonable.

One day, a crisis in my life, as so many others could say if they were relating their own story, was the day when I made up my mind not only to be Christ's, but to let others know it. I remember well the little old-fashioned chapel of the country church with its hard, straight-backed seats. I can remember now where I sat, though I was then scarcely thirteen years of age; and if I should tell you the whole truth I should have to confess that it was more than thirty years ago. I had no remarkable experience, no blinding light from heaven, no impulse that I could not resist if I had chosen to resist it; but I did know my duty and I determined, as a million boys have done before and since, to try to do it; and when the minister who had charge of that prayer-meeting, who was also my dear father, asked the question that so many ministers before and since have asked, whether there were any who were willing to acknowledge their love for Christ, for the first time I stood up, quite alone, if I remember rightly. I do not think I said a word, but that one night before all the people who were present committed me to the side of Christ.

I could also tell you, if you cared to read, of other events which have helped my spiritual life ; but they are all very simple, very commonplace, and appear tame enough when set down in black and white.   They have been simply efforts to help others, especially poor and sick people, in my parish or outside of it, and O ! how I wish these efforts had been recorded a thousand times oftener by the good angel as they might have been, had I always been ready to do every duty.   I should also tell you that I have found it necessary to have regular times for prayer and communion with Christ.   When these have been neglected, I am as confident as I am of my own existence, my spiritual life has suffered.

I pray that all readers of this account may grow from grace to grace, praying for each other as I am sure we will; that God will continually open new and larger spiritual treasures to each one of us.

FRANCIS E. CLARK.

BOSTON, MASS., 1896.

DETAINED FOR CONVERSION.

Rev. Dr. Cleveland related the following incident at the New York anniversary : In a revival of religion in
the church of which he was pastor, he
was visited one morning by a member
of his church, a widow, whose only
son was a sailor.   With a voice trem-
bling with emotion she said :

"Dr. Cleveland, I have called to
entreat you to join me in praying that
the wind may change."   He looked at
her in silent amazement.   "Yes," she

exclaimed earnestly, "my son has gone on board his vessel; they will sail to-night, unless the wind changes." "Well, Madam," said the Doctor, "I will pray that your son may be converted on this voyage; but to pray that God would alter the laws of the universe on his account, I fear is presumption." "Doctor," she replied, "my heart tells me differently. God's spirit is here, souls are being converted here. You have a meeting this evening, and if the wind should change, John would stay and go to it; and I believe if he went, he would be converted. Now, if you cannot join me, I must pray alone, for he must stay." "I will pray for his conversion," said the Doctor. On his way to the meeting, he glanced at the weather-vane ; to his surprise, the wind had changed, and it was blowing landward. On entering his crowded vestry, he soon observed John sitting upon the front seat. The young man seemed to drink in every word, rose to be prayed for, and attended the inquiry meeting. When he sailed from port, his mother's prayers had been answered ; he went a Christian.

PROFESSOR FRANCKE.

Professor Francke, of the University of Halle, like Chalmers, was a minister to others before his own heart was changed. He was about to preach from the words : "But these are written, that ye might believe that Jesus is the Christ, the Son of God, and that believing ye might have life through His name."

He says: "My whole former life came before my eyes just as one sees a whole city from a lofty spire. At first it seemed as if I could number all my sins! But soon there opened the great fountain of them—my own blind unbelief, which had so long deceived me. I was terrified with my lost condition, and wondered if God were merciful enough to bless me. Now I know Him; not alone as my God, but as my Father. All melancholy and unrest vanished, and I was so overcome with joy, that from the fullness of my heart I could praise my Saviour. With great sorrow I had kneeled, but with wonderful ecstasy I had risen up."

A few days afterwards he preached from the same text as before. The sermon was the first *real one* that he had preached. Henceforth his heart was in the work for which God had chosen him.

JOHN BUNYAN.

John Bunyan came to the first consciousness of his exceeding sinfulness,
by a reproof of a woman for his awful profanity—though she was a vile
sinner. He had a long and terrific
struggle with sin and unbelief before
his conversion. The following is an
outline account of his experience :

"Upon a day the good providence
of God called me to Bedford to work
at my calling ; and in one of the
streets of that town, I came where
there were three or four women sitting

at a door in the sun talking about the
things of God. And being now willing to hear what they said, I drew
near to hear their discourse, for I was
now a *brisk* talker of myself in the
matter of religion, but I say I heard,
but understood not ; for they were far
above out of my reach. Their talk
was about a new birth—the work of
God in their hearts, how God had visited their souls with His love in the
Lord Jesus. They reasoned of the
suggestions and temptations of Satan,
in particular ; and told to each other
by what means they had been af-
flicted, and how they were borne up
under his assaults. Methought they

7

spake as if joy did make them speak, they spake with such pleasantness of Scripture language, and with such appearance of grace in all they said, that they were to me as if I had found a new world. For I saw that in all my thoughts about religion and salvation, the new birth did never enter into my mind. I would often make it my business to be going again and again into the company of these poor people; for I could not stay away. Presently I found two things within me, at which I did sometimes marvel, the one was, a very great softness and tenderness of heart, which caused me to fall under conviction of what, by Scripture, they asserted; and the other was a great bending in my mind to a continual meditating on it, and on all good things, which at any time I heard or read of." Bunyan himself marveled, as he well might, at this childlike and angel-like turn of spirit, especially as he says : "Considering what a blind, ignorant, sordid, and ungodly wretch, but just before I was." His spirit softened like furrows under spring showers ; and like them, soon sent forth the "tender blade."

One of the first fruits of Bunyan's conversion, was a tender concern for those whom his former example had misled or hardened.

REV. ADONIRAM JUDSON.

AFTER finishing his university course, he became skeptical on theological studies, and strongly inclined to deism. He selected dramatic authorship as his profession during a brief period of time. He attached himself to a theatrical company for the purpose of becoming familiar with the regulations of the stage. The sudden death of a classmate under circumstances of peculiar interest, was the means of arresting his thoughts and putting him upon a course of serious examination of the claims of religion to his pesonal attention. While a transient guest at a public house, he was startled by hearing the sighs and groans of a very sick man in an adjoining apartment. On inquiry about the sufferer he was surprised to learn that it was his class-mate (an infidel), then dying. He sought his presence and was so im-pressed with the consciousness of a personal God and eternal life that he soon after became a hopeful Christian.

ATTORNEY-GENERAL GEORGE H. WILLIAMS.

At a recent Moody meeting in Portland, Oregon, ex-Attorney-General George H. Williams spoke with much feeling as follows : "I have made a great many speeches in my life, and some from this platform, but this is the first time I have ever spoken at a religious meeting. For months I have been troubled very much on the subject of Christianity. I have been looking forward to the meetings of Mr. Moody, and determined I would

attend them. When I first came I
thought I would sneak in and take a
back seat ; but I changed my mind
and said I would go on to the platform
and identify myself with these meetings. This I have done with the ex-
ception of one evening. This was the
first victory over my pride. Then,
yesterday, Mr. Moody came to my
house, and I joined with him in
prayer ; the first time I ever bowed
my knee to God or man in my life.
This was my second victory. Last
night I got up and asked the prayers
of God's people. This was my third
victory. I feel now perfectly satis-
fied ; the burden is rolled off and all

gone, and I feel that I could run or fly into the arms of Jesus Christ. This is my fourth victory. May God give us all strength to be true to our convictions!"

AUGUSTINE.

AUGUSTINE, the eminent scholar, and Bishop of Hippo, was the especial subject of his mother's prayers. Monica, his mother, was a most devout Christian. From her son's nineteenth to the twenty-eighth year of his age, while he was rolling in the filth of sin, did she in vigorous hope persist in earnest prayer. In his twenty-ninth year we find her still praying ; he left her and went to Rome ; bitterly she felt the separation, yet she returned to her former employment of prayer. From Rome he went to Milan, and there we find the praying mother again. At length the long-looked-for prayed-for time arrived. The teaching of Ambrose was blessed to her son's conversion, and the mother's happiness was completed.

BISHOP HUGH LATIMER.

Thomas Bilney was an ardent young convert, and longed to do something for his Lord and Master. Hugh Latimer was a zealous Roman Catholic priest, who preached against the Reformation. He berated Melancthon with great severity. Bilney went to him and told him that he wished to confess. In the privacy of the confessional he told him the whole burning story of conviction, conversion and new-found happiness. The Holy

Spirit helped, and from that hour Latimer gave his life to the cause he had before fought bitterly, and sealed his testimony with his blood. He never feared the face of man.

THE EMPEROR CONSTANTINE.

THE circumstances attending his conversion to Christianity are too familiar to most readers to render minute detail of them here necessary. No character has been exhibited to posterity in lights more contradictory than that of Constantine. Few things have occasioned more perplexity to writers of ecclesiastical history than his vision. According to his own account he was marching at the head of his army from France into Italy against Maxentius, on an expedition which he was fully aware involved in it his future destiny. Oppressed with extreme anxiety, and reflecting that he needed a force superior to arms for subduing the sorceries and magic of his adversary, he anxiously looked out for the aid of some deity, as that which alone could secure him success. About noon, when the sun began to decline, whilst praying for supernatural aid, a luminous cross was seen by the Emperor and his army, in the air above the sun, inscribed with the words : " BY THIS, CONQUER," at the sight of which amazement overpowered both himself and the soldiers

on the expedition with him. He continued to ponder on the event until
night, when, in a dream, the Author of
Christianity appeared to him to confirm
the vision, directing at the same time
to make the symbol of the cross his
military ensign. Constantine van-
quished his adversary, and no sooner
was he made master of Rome, than he
honored the cross by putting a spear
of that form into the hand of the
statue erected for him at Rome. His
religious zeal augmented with his
years. In his last illness he sum-
moned to the imperial palace at Ni-
conudia, several Christian bishops, fer-
vently requesting to receive from them

the ordinance of baptism and solemnly declared his intention of spending the remainder of his life as the disciple of Christ. He was accordingly baptized by Eusebius, bishop of that city, after which he entirely laid aside his purple and regal robe, and continued to wear a white garment till the day of his death, which after a short illness took place on the 22d of May, in the year 337, at the age of sixty-four, having reigned thirty-three years.

MRS. ADONIRAM JUDSON.

"It is just a year to-day," says Mrs. Judson, "since I entertained hope in Christ. About this time in the evening, when reflecting on the words of the lepers : 'If we enter into the city, then the famine is in the city, and we shall die there : if we sit still here we die also,' and felt that if I returned to the world I should surely perish, and I could but perish if I threw myself on the mercy of Christ. Then came light and relief and comfort such as I never knew before."

8

HE was an opulent merchant in the city of Lyons, where Christ had planted a numerous church, to serve as a pillar on which his truth was inscribed, or a candlestick on which he had placed the lamp of life. But the lamp had long been extinguished and the pillar removed. Lyons, in the time of Peter Waldo, was sunk into a state of the grossest darkness and superstition. At this time an extraordinary occurrence in providence was the means of

awakening the mind of Peter Waldo
to the one thing needful. One evening after supper, as he sat conversing
with a party of his friends and refresh-
ing himself among them, one of the
company fell down dead on the floor,
to the consternation of all who were
present. Such a lesson on the un-
certainty of human life most forcibly
arrested his attention. The sudden
death of his friend led him to think of
his own approaching dissolution, and
under the terrors of an awakened con-
science, he had recourse to the Holy
Scriptures for instruction and comfort.
There by Christ his Saviour he found
"the pearl of great price"—the way

of escape from the wrath to come.
Waldo was desirous of communicating
to others a portion of that happiness
which he himself enjoyed. He aban-
doned his mercantile pursuits, distributed his wealth to the poor as occasion required ; and while the latter
flocked to him to partake of his alms,
he labored to engage their attention to
the things which belonged to their everlasting peace. One of the first objects
of his pursuit, was to put into their
hands the word of life, and the in-
habitants of Europe were indebted to
him for the first translation of the
Bible into a modern tongue since the
time that the Latin had ceased to be

a living language—a gift of inestimable value. Amid great persecutions Peter Waldo led hundreds of thousands to know the truth as it is in Jesus, many of whom became martyrs for the truth, and their blood the seed of the church.

WILBERFORCE.

THE great English statesman, Wilberforce, was a gay *young* man, the delight of the clubs, and the joy of the Doncaster races. At the age of twenty, he was elected to the British Parliament, was sceptical in principles, and inclined to ridicule religion. He was convinced of his sins through the teaching of the Gospel by Dean Milner. His anguish for his sins was insupportable until he sought the counsel of good old John Newton, whom he had often heard preach. " Mr. Newton entered most kindly and affectionately into my case," said Wilberforce—and by his sympathy, instruction and advice he found peace with God.

DWIGHT L. MOODY.

(FULL CONSECRATION.)

" THIS blessing came upon me suddenly like a flash of lightning. It was in the fall of 1871. For months I had been hungering and thirsting for power in service. I had come to that point that I think I would have died if I had not got it. I remember I was walking the streets of New York. I had no more heart in the business I was about than if I had not belonged to this world at all. Right there in the

street the power of God came upon
me so wonderfully that I had to ask
God to stay his hand. I was filled
with a sense of God's goodness, and
felt as though I could take the whole
world to my heart. I took the old
sermon that I had preached before
without any power: it was the same
old truth, but there was a new power.
Many were impressed and converted.
This happened years after I was converted myself. I want to tell you this :
I would not for the whole world go
back to where I was before 1871.
Since then I have never lost the assurance that I am walking in communion with God, and I have a joy

in his service that sustains me and makes it easy work. I believe I was an older man then than I am now ; I have been growing younger ever since. I used to be very tired when preaching three times a week ; now I can preach five times a day and never get tired at all. I have done three times the work I did before, and it gets better and better every year. It is so easy to do a thing where love prompts you. It would be better, it seems to me, to go and break stone than to take to preaching in a professional spirit."

SAM W. SMALL.

"WELL, I was converted this way : The thirteenth day of last September (1883) I took my wife and children and went from Atlanta, my home, up to Cartersville, fifty miles away, to hear Sam Jones preach in a big camp-meeting. It was a kind of a Sunday excursion. There had been no change of life up to that time—but for the worse. I heard Sam Jones preach and I was convicted of my sins. I was

awakened. This was on Sunday. I
went home and got drunk and stayed
drunk until Tuesday afternoon. Then
I went into my library at about four
o'clock and I prayed until I felt that I
saw my way clear. I had been think-
ing about my condition and I felt that
the time had come to stop. I was
getting over my depth. I looked the
whole thing in the face and I sur-
rendered to the Lord. Then I went
and had 3,000 circulars printed, an-
nouncing that I would preach that
evening at the corner of Marietta and
Peachtree streets. The first job-
printer that I went to thought I was
crazy. You see I had been on a

drunk, and my friends had often thought that I would go crazy from drink, and so this man thought the same, and wouldn't print my bills. So I went to another place and got them printed at last. I had them distributed, and at the place mentioned a great crowd assembled when it came time for me to speak. I told them what had happened, what I was going to do, and told them I meant business. They could stand off and see me do it. Then as soon as Jones had heard what had happened, he telegraphed me to come up to Cartersville and speak for him. Well, I preached the next two nights in local churches, and

Saturday I went up and preached for
Jones. From that day to this I have
lost about a dozen days, speaking
some days from one to four times."

MRS. MARGUERITE BOTTOME.

I HAD not what would be called a wonderful Christian conversion. When fourteen years of age I attended revival meetings in the Sands Street Methodist Episcopal Church of Brooklyn. I became deeply interested in the earnest appeals made to seek the Lord Jesus Christ. For six weeks I went to the altar with others seeking forgiveness of my sins. All my young friends were converted. Yet I could not feel that my sins were forgiven.

127

I felt very sadly and wept much of the time, for I wanted to obtain peace with God. It was all emotional feeling with me and wore off in school associations and did not return until I was brought under the influence of some appeals from the pulpit or hymn sung, such songs as "Come Ye Sinners, Poor and Needy."

But at last the superintendent of our Sunday-school expressed to me the simplicity of faith, and I grasped the idea that God was my father and that Christ was my loving brother. I called on His name, and I have peace and joy and the assurance of my sins forgiven. It is true I had turned to-

wards God in faith; but the feeling
soon passed away, and then I thought,
"I have deceived myself." Doubts
gathered over me and then deep
trouble commenced, for I was conscious that I was regarded as one of
the converts. I had joined the church
class and attended its meetings regu-
larly and yet black clouds of doubt
gathered over me. When the time
came for the probationers to be received into the church, this question
was asked of all: "Have you reason
to believe that God for Christ's sake has
forgiven your sins?" All the members
of the class by my side said, "Yes!"
I said "No," because I did not then

feel, as I did before, that my sins were forgiven. I now regard this as a period of doubt and temptation. I continued to be faithful to do my duty as I could see it in church relations and gradually light and confirmation of faith beamed into my soul. I found my heart longing to love and serve the Lord Jesus, and I gradually, by witnessing for Him and seeking to do His will, came from the vestibule of faith into a large place of liberty. At this time of life I am impressed with the importance of not emphasizing too strongly the emotional element in teaching seekers after the Truth and light, but to urge simple trust in Christ and anchorage in God's promise, tested and proved by faith, prayer and service in His name. Light will beam on some suddenly like a sunburst, and others like the gray dawn gradually into clear light.

PART II.

THE GLEANER.

WITH INTRODUCTORY STORIES ILLUSTRATIVE

OF THE TRIUMPHS OF FAITH,

PRAYER AND SERVICE.

THE LIGHTHOUSE IN THE STORM.

FOR several months we have had as a member of our Society a man in middle life, who by his earnestness and sincere Christian purpose has added very much to the spiritual power of our meetings. He has more than once given testimony to the grace of God in reaching him, while he was in the midst of a life of sin. We have heard from his own lips the substance of the story of his conversion, as lately more fully given by him in the Cremorne Mission, in New York City.

He said ; "I thank God that He led me into this mission one night and caused me to give my heart to Him. Drink and sin robbed me of as beautiful a family as a father ever had, and finally placed me in a felon's cell. I remember how in a distant city I was led handcuffed by the door of the very house where once I had lived a very respectable man, and it seemed as though my heart would break; that was one of the ways that God took to lead me to himself. Finally I came to New York, and here I sank as low as it was possible to get in sin. The place where I lived was nothing but the abode of thieves. But praise God ! He has taken sin away from me. I am a drunkard no longer. I am a criminal no more. God has taken away all profanity from me and has made my life bright and hopeful. Although it is a continual struggle with the power of sin, yet I am sure God is going to be the victor and is the victor to-night."

About ten days ago I received a letter from this man, telling me that he has decided to give his services and life to God ; that he expects to become a worker in some city mission ; and adding this word: " I have found plenty to do for God thus far and have been abundantly rewarded, and I am sure that a door will be opened somewhere soon for work or for preparation for it."

FRANCIS STODDARD HAINES,

Of Christian Endeavor Society

First Presbyterian Church,

Easton, Pa.,

February, 3, 1896.

A WORD FOR CHRIST.

I WISH I might do some little service," said C—— one Sabbath afternoon in February, 1894.

"O God, show me," said he in silent prayer, "what I can do."

Leaving home that evening the thought came to him, "I will ask Halsey P—— to become an associate member of the Endeavor Society."

Halsey was a fireman on the local railroad, but not a Christian. C—— called on his friend; the associate pledge was finally signed, and Halsey received into the society.

At the next consecration meeting, instead of answering " present " to his name, Halsey arose and said that he desired to take an open stand for Christ, and with God's help, proposed to do so then.

On Easter Sunday, he was baptized into the church, and from that day on, his short life was one of growing activity and joy in the Master's service. He neglected no opportunity to speak for his Master. The Y. M. C. A., the church prayer-meeting, the Endeavor Society, became to him joyous means of grace and of service.

On the morning of July 19, as he kissed the dear wife and two-weeks' old baby boy, good-bye, he said : " Wife, dear, I hope we may have a good run to-day, so that I can go to prayer-meeting to-night.

The home run from A—— was that of the fast express. As the train was dashing through the little village of E——, it suddenly swept into an open switch upon which two freight cars were standing. The emergency brake saved the train, but engineer and fireman lost their lives.

When they brought the mangled body of the fireman home, C—— look-ing into the casket with streaming eyes thanked God for guiding him to speak a word which saved a soul.

CHARLES C. PIERCE,

Of Christian Endeavor Society,

First Baptist Church,

Oneonta, N. Y.

Feb. 19, 1896.

ANSWERS OF PRAYER.

It was at the beginning of a session of the Sunday school of which I was superintendent a few years since, that word came from a messenger of the near approach of death to one of the scholars that I loved very. much. She was a sweet little girl, bright and sunny, and was particularly gifted in recitation. Many times she had thrilled our hearts with her verses. It scarcely seemed possible that Ida was so near leaving us. With the message came the request for prayers ; that God would spare her to that home where she was loved so dearly. Afterward I learned the physician had just left the house, and said : "It is of no use to do anything further ; we have done all that medicines can do, she will live at the most only a few hours." It was a case of Bright's disease, so deadly in its effects, and so sure in its results.

The mind was dulled for a moment, but quickly responded to the thought of the power of God in such an extremity. After the opening exercises a statement of the case was made to the school, and the request made for all to pray. The child was known to nearly every one in the room, and there must have been a large volume of prayer that went in those moments to the Throne. I was particularly impressed, as I prayed, to believe my prayer and the prayers of the school, were certainly carried by angel bands to the mercy seat, for at that very time a change came in the sufferer. The face brightened, returning power was seen, and the feeble body seemed renewed by God Himself. If she did not literally rise up and walk she was restored to health, and was soon in her place in the school, and lives to-day a mark of God's mercy.

WALTER I. SOUTHERTON,

Of Christian Endeavor Society,

Baptist Temple,

Brooklyn,

March 4, 1896.

GUIDED THROUGH A CLOUD.

" I would ye should understand, brethren, that the things which happened unto me have fallen out rather unto the furtherance of the gospel."

Phil. 1 : 12.

I was in a hospital in Madras, India. One short year had been spent in the land of my adoption, among the people of my love, *my* people. Now the deadly fever had me in its toils, and the physicians had agreed, " You must go home. It is the only hope of prolonging your life."

Go home ? Was not this my home ?

Prolonging my life? That was not what I sought. I had rather a thousand-fold work out my little day in India, however brief, and die among my people, at my post, than live the longest life in America.

But finally when He had quieted my heart to talk it all over with Him, He plainly showed me that my life was not my own, and that I dared not sacrifice what belonged to Him, unless He required it. Then I said, "Thy will is always sweet. I will go." And from the prison-house of my affliction, still groaning beneath the cruel bonds of blighted hopes, defeated purposes, frustrated life-ambitions, I was able to appropriate the message of Paul to his Philippian brethren.

Its fulfilment only waited my landing in America. In the mail awaiting me was a letter from Mrs. L. D. Osborn, Principal of the Union Missionary Training Institute of Brooklyn, urging me to take her place in the school, for she was ill and must relinquish the work, and saying there was no one else whom she believed to be so qualified of God. Then I knew why the call home. Verily it was for the furtherence of the Gospel. Thus from the field of my own individual efforts for India's evangelization I was led to the sphere of multiplying myself in the training of the many who are now scattering to earth's ends.

HESTER ALWAY.

Baptist Young Peoples' Union,
        Washington Ave. Bap. Ch.
            Brooklyn, N. Y.
   April 6, 1896.

SYMPATHY IN THE STORM.

THE following incident is not more remarkable than many experienced by a multitude of persons engaged in Christian work : and that the writer has experienced in a variety of ways. But it is a marked illustration of the effectiveness of a word in time.

At eight o'clock in the evening of a blustering February day, in 1894, I was in a gentleman's furnishing store on Fulton Street, Brooklyn, conversing with the proprietor. A man about thirty-five years of age came in the store and asked the proprietor if he would give him sufficient change to pay for a night's lodging. He said he had eaten nothing since morning, and felt ill. He was evidently somewhat under the influence of liquor, but not drunken. The proprietor refused to help him. I turned to him and said, "If I give you sufficient amount of money for supper and a lodging, will you promise me on your honor that you will not spend any of it for liquor?" I then took his hand and said, "I sympathize with you in your trial; you are comparatively a young man and if you will resolve by

God's help you can conquer this habit ;
but you will have a battle before you,
and must exercise all the courage and
decision you can summon. I shall
trust your honor in helping you. Will
you ask God to help you? Do you
truly promise me that you will do
your best to keep your word now ;
this may be a turning-point in your
life." He said, "Before God I promise you." I gave him sufficient
amount of money for the purpose,
and said, "Will you call at my house
to-morrow at nine o'clock and tell me
if you have kept your word, and I
will see about further help." The
next morning he was at my house at

the time appointed ; his face was all aglow with good cheer. He said, " After I received the money, my thirst came on me, and I fought it off. I never touched a drop ; I feel so encouraged, for I have won a battle, and am determined to be a man." In a word, he reformed, soon confessed conversion to Christ, and obtained a position in business and, when fully established in strength, wrote me that the words and deeds of cheer in the store, by God's grace, had saved him.

ARTHUR CLARK,

Y. M. C. A. of Brooklyn,
    March 4, 1897.

THE GIFT AND THE GIVER.

For some time—after opening the Door of Hope for those so laid upon my heart to rescue,—while praying for the needs of the work, the $15,000 mortgage resting upon the property would often come to mind. For lack of faith, however, it was generally not dwelt upon and though the semi-yearly interest due upon it was always granted in answer to prayer, the amount itself was not really committed to God for removal as it should have been.

Last summer, most unexpectedly, the inconsistency of this presented itself to me, and a burden of prayer seemed pressing upon my heart, concerning the matter; finally, after much waiting before the Lord, I could not but feel it would be more pleasing to Him to have this wiped out, and therefore asked for sufficient faith to *believe* for its removal, before the time it would have to be renewed. This was granted; and, with thanksgiving and praise I took the necessary amount most definitely when thus engaged in prayer.

At first, I was tempted quietly to be still and see if this expectation would be met, but instantly upon reflection came the suggestion that that was *sight*, not *faith* : for " Faith was the *substance* of things hoped for, and the evidence of things not seen," (Heb. 11 : 1), therefore such proceedings would not glorify God if I truly believed. Nor can I feel to this day that it would have been honoring Him to have proclaimed this Faith-Gift of money abroad, as it would necessarily have assumed a form of an appeal to those who listened and sooner or later possibly induced many to contribute towards its liquidation. Besides, it would have been acknowledging a *need* which existed, in a most forcible manner, and, from the opening of the

Home God has never permitted me any freedom to obtain funds in this way. I would truly rather *trust* for every requirement connected with the home, than to have our wants supplied through the usual methods of solicitations, as personally it has taught me more of the reality and readiness of God in answering believing prayer than anything in my Christian experience before. I felt directed to talk over the subject of the debt with two intimate friends, knowing well that the confidence thus entrusted would never be misunderstood nor misplaced— often making the assertion in a somewhat positive way, that the mortgage

would never have to be resumed after
the following June ; for a moment or
so they regarded me with concern.
Reading their looks, particularly as
one of them went on to say quite
gravely, that "it was quite a large
sum, and perhaps I did not fully real-
ize the amount and the shortness of
the time before it would expire."

Resting in God I quickly responded :
"Well, you will see when we meet
next summer, every cent will be can-
celled," though I had not the faintest
idea where a dollar of it was coming
from.   No sooner had these words
been uttered than the conscious sense
of having pleased God gave me such

a delightful rest and assurance that He would deliver.

Within the past two weeks this claim was again upheld privately in prayer and praise in my own room, and one day (Jan. 13), a dear friend asked me to grant her a little time, as she had some most important matters to talk over with me. I had not the faintest idea what she intended talking about until she explained it was in connection with the Door of Hope.

Being seated, my surprise was great when she questioned me concerning the mortgage, and said she wished to know the *exact* amount. On answering, immediately an unexplainable look crossed her beautiful countenance which caused my heart to give a big throb of joy, and the thought flashed through my mind that possibly she was going to give me a thousand dollars towards it. I therefore was by *no means* prepared for the next remark, which was : "I have talked this matter over with no one, therefore am only influenced by God, and I believe He would have me on one condition, that my name be withheld, just sit down now and draw you a check for $15,000, to wipe it out forever."

The feelings of gratitude, first to God and then to the noble-hearted donor, can *never* be expressed, for it meant so much to me of my Lord. Not one dollar of it had been solicited. "simply prompted," as she informed me, by the Holy Spirit when in prayer; and, in being made willing to do this, she was glad to so hide behind the "Master" in the gift, that He might receive the praise and be seen *alone* through it all. Dear reader, will you not take your burden in prayer and faith to Jesus? Just insist on an answer.

Mrs. E. M. Whittemore,

Door of Hope,

New York,

www.ingramcontent.com/pod-product-compliance
Lightning Source LLC
Chambersburg PA
CBHW020017030726
47500CB00002B/629